AF293135

 tredition®

tredition was established in 2006 by Sandra Latusseck and Soenke Schulz. Based in Hamburg, Germany, tredition offers publishing solutions to authors and publishing houses, combined with worldwide distribution of printed and digital book content. tredition is uniquely positioned to enable authors and publishing houses to create books on their own terms and without conventional manufacturing risks.

For more information please visit: www.tredition.com

TREDITION CLASSICS

This book is part of the TREDITION CLASSICS series. The creators of this series are united by passion for literature and driven by the intention of making all public domain books available in printed format again - worldwide. Most TREDITION CLASSICS titles have been out of print and off the bookstore shelves for decades. At tredition we believe that a great book never goes out of style and that its value is eternal. Several mostly non-profit literature projects provide content to tredition. To support their good work, tredition donates a portion of the proceeds from each sold copy. As a reader of a TREDITION CLASSICS book, you support our mission to save many of the amazing works of world literature from oblivion. See all available books at www.tredition.com.

Project Gutenberg

The content for this book has been graciously provided by Project Gutenberg. Project Gutenberg is a non-profit organization founded by Michael Hart in 1971 at the University of Illinois. The mission of Project Gutenberg is simple: To encourage the creation and distribution of eBooks. Project Gutenberg is the first and largest collection of public domain eBooks.

A String of Amber Beads

Martha Everts Holden

Imprint

This book is part of TREDITION CLASSICS

Author: Martha Everts Holden
Cover design: Buchgut, Berlin – Germany

Publisher: tredition GmbH, Hamburg - Germany
ISBN: 978-3-8424-8306-4

www.tredition.com
www.tredition.de

Copyright:
The content of this book is sourced from the public domain.

The intention of the TREDITION CLASSICS series is to make world literature in the public domain available in printed format. Literary enthusiasts and organizations, such as Project Gutenberg, world-wide have scanned and digitally edited the original texts. tredition has subsequently formatted and redesigned the content into a modern reading layout. Therefore, we cannot guarantee the exact reproduction of the original format of a particular historic edition. Please also note that no modifications have been made to the spelling, therefore it may differ from the orthography used today.

DEDICATED

TO

THE LATE

ANDREW SHUMAN

MY LITERARY ADVISER

AND

TRUEST FRIEND

CONTENTS.

A STRING OF BEADS

I.

"I DIDN'T THINK."

"I didn't think!" A woman flings the whiteness of her reputation in the dust, and, waking to the realization of her loss when the cruel glare of the world's disapproval reveals it, she seeks to plead her thoughtlessness as an entreaty of the world's pardon. But the flint-hearted world is slow to grant it, if she be a woman. "You have thrown your rose in the dust, go live there with it," the world cries, and there is no appeal, although the dust become the grave of all that is bright and lovely and sweet in a thoughtless woman's really innocent life. A young girl flirts with a stranger on the street. The result is something disagreeable, and straight-way comes the excuse: "Why, I didn't think! I meant no harm; I just wanted to have a little fun." Now, look me straight in the eye, young gossamer-head, while I tell you what I *know*. The girl who will flirt with strange men in public places, however harmless and innocent it may appear, places herself in that man's estimation upon a level with the most abandoned of her sex and courts the same regard. Strong language, perhaps you think, but I tell you it is gospel truth, and I feel like going into orders and preaching from a pulpit whenever I see a thoughtless, gay and giddy girl tiptoeing her way upon the road that leads direct to destruction. The boat that dances like a feather on the current a mile above Niagara's plunge is just as much lost as when it enters the swirling, swinging wrath of waters, unless some strong hand head it up stream and out of danger. A flirtation to-day is a ripple merely, but to-morrow it will be a breaker, and then a whirlpool, and after that comes hopeless loss of character. Girls, I have seen you gather up your roses from their vases at night and fold them away in damp paper to protect their loveliness for another day. I have seen you pluck the jewels like sun sparkles from your fingers and your ears, and lay them in velvet caskets which you locked with a silver key for safe beeping. You do all this for flowers which a thousand suns shall duplicate in beauty, and for jewels for which a handful of dollars can reimburse your loss; but you are infinitely careless with the delicate rose of maidenliness, which, once faded, no summer shining can ever woo back to freshness, and with the unsullied jewel of personal reputation which all the wealth of kings can never buy back again, once lost. See to it that you preserve that modesty and womanliness without which the prettiest girl in the world is no better than a bit of scentless lawn in a milliner's window, as compared to the white rose in the garden, around which the honey bees gather. See to it that you lock up the unsullied splendor of the jewel of your reputation as carefully as you do your diamonds, and carry the key within your heart of hearts.

II.

"STAY WHERE YOU ARE."

I received a letter the other day in which the writer said: "Amber, I want to come to the city and earn my living. What chance have I?" And I felt like posting back an immediate answer and saying: "Stay where you are." I didn't do it, though, for I knew it would be useless. The child is bound to come, and come she will. And she will drift into a third-rate Chicago boarding-house, than which if there is anything meaner—let us pray! And if she is pretty she will have to carry herself like snow on high hills to avoid contamination. If she is confiding and innocent the fate of that highly persecuted heroine of old-fashioned romance, Clarissa Harlowe, is before her. If she is homely the doors of opportunity are firmly closed against her. If she is smart she will perhaps succeed in earning enough money to pay her board bill and have sufficient left over to indulge in the maddening extravagance of an occasional paper of pins or a ball of tape! What if, after hard labor, and repeated failure, she does secure something like success? No sooner will she do so, than up will step some dapper youth who will beckon her over the border into the land where troubles just begin. She won't know how to sew, or bake, or make good coffee, for such arts are liable to be overlooked when a girl makes a career for herself, and so love will gallop away over the hills like a riderless steed, and happiness will flare like a light in a windy night. Oh, no, my little country maid, stay where you are, if you have a home and friends. Be content with fishing for trout in the brook rather than cruising a stormy sea for whales. A great city is a cruel place for young lives. It takes them as the cider press takes juicy apples, sun-kissed and flavored with the breath of the hills, and crushes them into pulp. There is a spoonful of juice for each apple, but cider is cheap!

III.

A COWARDLY MATE.

I know a wife who is waiting, safe and sound in her father's home, for her young husband to earn the money single handed to make a home worthy of her acceptance. She makes me think of the first mate of a ship who should stay on shore until the captain tested the ability of his vessel to weather the storm. Back to your ship, you cowardly one! If the boat goes down, go down with it, but do not count yourself worthy of any fair weather you did not help to gain! A woman who will do all she can to win a man's love merely for the profit his purse is going to be to her, and will desert him when the cash runs low, is a bad woman and carries a bad heart in her bosom. Why, you are never really wedded until you have had dark days together. What earthly purpose would a cable serve that never was tested by a weight? Of what use is the tie that binds wedded hearts together if like a filament of floss it parts when the strain is brought to bear upon it? It is not when you are young, my dear, when the skies are blue and every wayside weed flaunts a summer blossom, that the story of your life is recorded. It is when "Darby and Joan" are faded and wasted and old, when poverty has nipped the roses, when trouble and want and care have flown like uncanny birds over their heads (but never yet nested in their hearts, thank God), that the completed chronicle of their lives furnishes the record over which heaven smiles or weeps.

IV.

THEY CARRY NO BANNER.

There never yet was a grand procession that was not accompanied, or, rather, in great measure made up of, followers and onlookers. So in this life parade of ours, with its ever varying pageant and brilliant display, there are comparatively few who carry banners, who disport the epaulette, and the gold lace. And sometimes, we who help swell the ranks of those who watch and wait, grow discouraged, almost thinking that life is a failure because it holds no gala-day for us, nothing but sober tints and quiet duties. What chance for any one, and a woman especially, to make a career for herself, tied down to a lot of precious babies, or lassooed by ten thousand galloping cares! As well expect a rose to blossom in mid-winter hedges, or a lark to sing in a snowstorm, as to look for bloom and song in such a life! But just bend down your ear a minute, poor, tired, overworked and troubled sister, I have a special word for you. It is simply impossible for circumstances of any sort to overthrow the high spirit of one who believes in something yet to come and out of sight. What are poverty and adverse fate and mocking hopes and disappointed ambition to the soul which is only journeying through an unfriendly world to a heritage that cannot fail? As well might a flower complain of the rains that called it from the sod, of the winds that rocked it, and the cloudless noons that flamed above it, when June at last has lightly laid the coronal of summer's perfect bloom upon its bending bough. We shall find our June somewhere, never fear. Be content then a little longer with uncongenial surroundings and a life that knows no outlook of hope. Be all the sweeter and the stronger and the braver that the way is short. To-morrow, in the Palace of Love, the dark and unfriendly inn that sheltered us for a night upon the way, shall be forgotten.

V.

SHUT IN.

Were you ever shut in by a fog? Lost at mid-day in a soundless, rayless world of nebulous vapor—so seemingly alone in the universe that your voice found no echo, and your ears caught no footfall in all the vast domain of silence about you? The other morning, when I left the house, I paused in wonderment at the strange world into which I was about to plunge. All landmarks were gone, nothing but silver and gray left of nature's brilliant tints, not even so much shadow as an artist might use to accentuate a bird's wing in crayon—no heaven above, no earth beneath. The interior of a raised biscuit could not have been more densely uniform than the atmosphere. It seemed as if the world had slipped its moorings and drifted off its course into companionless space, leaving me behind, as an ocean steamer sometimes leaves a straggler on an uninhabited shore. I felt like sending forth a call that should give my bearings and bring back a boat to the rescue. I groped my way down the steps, and, following an intuition, sought the station. Ahead of me I heard muffled steps, yet saw no form. But suddenly a doorway opened in the east and out strode the sun. In the air above and about me, behold, the wonder of diamond domes and slender minarets traced in pearl! The wayside banks were fringed with crystal spray of downbeaten weed and bush that sparkled like the billows of a sunlit sea. The tall elms here and there towered like the masts of returning ships, slow sailing from a wintry voyage back to summer lands and splendor. There was no sound in all the air, but the whole universe seemed singing as when the morning stars chorused the glory of God. More and more widely opened that doorway in the east; step by step advanced the great magician, and over all the world the splendor grew, until it seemed too much for mortal eyes to bear, when lo! a touch dispelled it all and commonplace day stood revealed.

VI.

THE CIRCLING YEAR — A CLOCK.

The circling year is a clock whereon nature writes the hours in blossoms. First come the wind flowers and the violets, they denote the early morning hours and are quickly passed. The forenoon is marked by lilacs, apple blooms and roses. The day's meridian is reached with lilies, red carnations, and the dusky splendor of pansies and passion flowers. Then come the languid poppy and the prim little 4 o'clock, the marigold, the sweet pea, and later the dahlia and the many-tinted chrysanthemum to mark the day's decline. Lastly the goldenrod, the aster and the gentian, tell us it is evening time, and night and frost are close at hand. The rose hour has struck already for '93. The garden beds are full of scattered petals and the dusty roadways glimmer with ghostly blossoms too wan to be roses, and wafted by a breath into nothingness. With such a calendar to mark the advance of decay and death the seasons differ from the mortal race which substitutes aches and pains for a horologe of flowers, and grows old by processes of physical failure and mental blight.

VII.

SOMETHING BETTER THAN SURFACE MANNERS.

There are days when my heart is so full of love for young girls that as I pass them on the street I feel myself smiling as one does to walk by a garden of daffodils. And when I see how careful some of them are to be circumspect and demure, I think to myself how fine a thing it is, to be sure, to have good manners! How happy the parent whose young daughter knows just how to hold her hands in company, just how and when to smile, just how to enter a room or gracefully leave it. Easy, indeed, must lie the head of that mother who is secure in the knowledge that her daughter will never make a false step in the stately minuet of etiquette, or strike a discordant note in the festival of life; that she will never laugh too loud, nor turn her head in the street, even when the gay and glittering "king of the cannibal isles" rides by, nor do anything odd or queer or unconventional. To the mother who believes that good manners can be taught in books and conned in dancing schools, there is something to satisfy the heart's finest craving in a strictly conventional daughter, who thinks and acts and speaks by rule, and whose life is like the life of an apricot, canned, or a music box wound up with a key. But to my thinking, my dear, good manners are not put on and off like varying fashions, nor done up like sweetmeats, pound for pound, and kept in the storeroom for state occasions. They strike root from the heart out, and the prettiest manners in the world are only the blossoming of a good heart. Surface manners are like cut flowers stuck in a shallow glass with just enough water to keep them fresh an hour or so, but the courtesy that has its growth in the heart is like the rosebush in the garden that no inclement season can kill, and no dark day force to forego the unfolding of a bud.

VIII.

MIND YOUR OWN BUSINESS.

I am more and more convinced the longer I live that the very best advice that was ever given from friend to friend is contained in those four words: "Mind your own business." The following of it would save many a heartache. Its observance would insure against every sort of wrangling. When we mind our own business we are sure of success in what we undertake, and may count upon a glorious immunity from failure. When the husbandman harvests a crop by hanging over the fence and watching his neighbor hoe weeds, it will be time for you and for me to achieve renown in any undertaking in which we do not exclusively mind our own business. If I had a family of young folks to give advice to, my early, late and constant admonition would be always and everywhere to "mind their own business." Thus should they woo harmony and peace, and live to enjoy something like the completeness of life.

IX.

THE PEOPLE WHO MAKE ME MOST WEARY.

In the ups and downs and hithers and thithers of an eventful life shall I tell you the people who have made me the most weary? It is not the bad people, nor the foolish people; we can get along with all such because of a streak of common humanity in us all, but I cannot survive without extreme lassitude the decorous people; those who slip through life without sound or sparkle, those who behave themselves upon every occasion, and would pass through a dynamite explosion without rumpling a hair; those who never have done anything out of the way and never will, simply for the same reason that a fish cannot perspire—no blood in 'em! Cut them and they would run cold sap, like a maple tree in April. Such people are always frightened to death for fear of what the world is going to say about them. They are under everlasting bonds to keep the peace. I wonder that they ever un-bend to kiss their children. If one of them lived in my house I should stick pins in him. Morality and goodness that lie no deeper than "behavior" are like the veneering they put on cheap tables—very tawdry and soon peeled off.

X.

NOTHING SO GRAND AS FORCE.

Reading about the superb management of the big fire the other day, a certain girl of my acquaintance remarked: "Is there anything so grand in a man as force? In my estimation those firemen and the chief who so splendidly controlled them are as far superior to the dancing youth, we meet at parties and hops, as meat is better than foam." Put that into your pipe, you callow striplings, who aim to be lady-killers! It is not your tennis suits, nor your small feet, nor your ability to dance and lead the german that makes a woman's heart kindle at your approach. It is your response to an emergency, your muscle in a tilt against odds, your endurance and force, that will win the way to feminine regard. As for me there is something pathetic in the sight of a big, handsome fellow in dancing pumps and a Prince Albert coat. I would rather see him swinging a blacksmith's hammer, or driving a plow through stony furrows if need be. The "original man" was not created to shine in the military schottische or win his laurels in the berlin.

XI.

A RAINY RHAPSODY.

Gently, idly, lazily, as petals from an over-blown rose, while I write, the welcome rain is falling. The sky is neutral tinted, save in the east, where a faint blush lingers. All along the country roadways a thousand fainting clovers uplift their purple crests, and in the dusky spaces of the dense June woods a host of grateful leaves wait and beckon. A voice comes from the garden bed; it is the complaint of the pansy. "Here I lie," it says, "with all my jewels low in the dust. Where is the purple of my amethysts, the yellow of my topaz, the inimitable sheen of my milk-white pearls? Alas and alack for pansies when the rain beats them earthward!" The marigold, like a yellow-haired boy with his straw hat well back from his flying mane, whistles softly to himself for joy, and buries his hands in the pockets of his green breeches. The peonies burn low their tinted globes of light, and the sweet peas swing like idle girls upon the tendrils of their drooping vines. The dog lifts his nose and sniffs the moist air approvingly, while poor Old Tom, the cat, blinks benignly upon the scene. In the poultry yard the hens pose in the same indescribable amaze that has bewildered their species since the dawn of time. I think the first chicken that was ever hatched in Eden must have experienced some great nervous shock that has descended along the infinite line of its progeny. The monotonous rooster chants ever and anon from the top of the fence his unalterable convictions. The ducks waddle waggishly through the rain and the pigeons coo softly the mellowest melodies that ever sounded from a feathered throat.

XII.

CAUSE FOR WONDER.

I do not wonder so much that so few people blossom into sunny old age, as I wonder that one-half of humanity ever shows a leaf or unfolds a bud. Look at the idiots who have children. Look at the little ones thrown into the street like troublesome kittens. Look at the injudicious methods of diet and training. I declare, my dear, if I were to go into the room where Theodore Thomas was rehearsing his orchestra, and see the flutists using their flutes for hammers, and the violinists using their violins for tennis rackets, and the divine old cello in the hands of a lusty blacksmith who was utilizing it for an anvil, the sight would be nothing to what it is to see the muddle we make of the children's sweet lives. God meant us for musical instruments, and gave to each soul its capacity for some original harmony. Can a flute keep its tone for three score years it you use it for a clothes stick on wash day, or a violin retain intact the angel voice within it if you let rats breed and nest in it, fling it against the side of the house and dance on it with hob-nailed boots? If an instrument subjected to such usage pipes out a silver note once in a dozen years, uncover your head when you hear it, for it is the original angel within the mechanism, which nothing can kill!

XIII.

THE FIRST KATYDID.

The first katydid of the season has whipped out his bow and drawn the preparatory note across the strings of his violin. He is alone at present and he plays to an empty house, but it will not be long before the orchestra fills up and the music is in full blast. The cricket is getting ready to throw aside the green baize that has held his piccolo so long, and before the middle of the month there will not be a tuft of grass nor a shelter of low-lying leaves that is not alive with the shrill, complaining sweetness of his theme. The goldenrod has lighted the candles in the candelabra that skirt the borders of the wood, and the aster has already hung out her purple gown and her yellow laces upon the bushes that follow the windings of the steep ravine. Only six weeks to frost! Only six weeks to the time for the unbottling of the year's vintage and the exchange of tea for sparkling wine. Hasten forward, then, oh, days of radiant life and sparkling weather! We are tired of torrid waves and flies; of snakes, hornets and cyclones.

XIV.

A PLEA FOR MEN.

A more or less extended experience as a bread-winner has taught me a noble charity for men. I used to think that all the head of a family was good for was to accumulate riches and pay bills, but I am beginning to think that there is many a martyr spirit hidden away beneath the business man's suit of tweed. Wife and daughters stand ever before him, like hoppers waiting for grist to grind. "Give! Give!" is their constant cry, like the rattle of the upper and nether stones. This panegyric does not apply to the man who frequents clubs and spends his money on between-meal drinks and lottery tickets. It applies rather to the unselfish, hardworking father of a family, who works early and late to keep his daughters like lilies that have no need to toil, and to help maintain the ostentation of vain display upon which depends the social success of a worldly and frivolous wife. It would be far more to those daughters' credit if they did something in the line of honest and honorable toil to support themselves, rather than live on the heart's blood of an unselfish and overworked father; and as for the wife who exacts the income of a duchess to keep up the silly parade of Vanity Fair, there may come a day for her, when, shorn of the generous and loving support of a good husband, and forced to earn her own livelihood, as the penniless widows of bankrupt men are sometimes forced to do, she will appreciate, too late, the blessing that Heaven has taken from her.

XV.

WHAT I'M TIRED OF.

I am tired of many things. I am tired of the miserable little god, "worry," shrined in every home. I am tired of doing perpetual homage to the same black-faced little wretch. I am tired of putting down pride and curbing a righteous indignation. I am tired of keeping my hands off human weeds. I am tired of crucifying my tastes, and cultivating the nickel that springs perennial to meet my needs. I am tired of poverty and all needful discipline. I am tired of seeing babies born to people who don't know how to bring them up. I am tired of folks who smile continuously. I am tired of amiable fools and the platitudes of unintelligent saints. I am tired of mediocrity. I am tired of cats, both human and feline. I am tired of being a soldier and marching with the advance guard. I am tired of girls who giggle and of boys who swear. I am tired of married women who think it charming to be a little giddy, and of married men who ogle young girls and other men's wives. I am tired of a world where love is like the blossom of the century plant, unfolding only once in a hundred years. I am tired of men who are worthless and decayed to the core, like blighted peaches. I am tired of seeing such men in power. I am tired of being obliged to smile where I long to smite. I am tired of vulgarity which glides forever through the world like the snake through Eden. I am tired of women who bear the hearts of tigers, and of men who roar like lions, yet show the valor of mice. I am tired of living shoulder to shoulder with my pet antipathies. I am tired of the everlasting inveighing against capital, when any idiot knows that capital is the king-bolt that holds the world together. I am tired of wearing shabby clothes, and meeting folks who judge of a parcel by the quality of wrapping paper it is incased in. I am tired of being well-behaved and decorous when I want to fling stones and make faces. I am tired of smelling the game dinner of my neighbor and sitting down at home to beans and bacon. I am tired of many more things, the enumeration of which would take from now until the day after forever.

XVI.

NOTHING LIKE A GOOD LAUGH.

Do you know, my dear, that there is absolutely nothing that will help you to bear the ills of life so well as a good laugh. Laugh all you can, and the small imps in blue who love to preempt their quarters in a human heart will scatter away like owls before the music of flutes. There are few of the minor difficulties and annoyances that will not dissipate at the charge of the nonsense brigade. If the clothes line breaks, if the cat tips over the milk and the dog elopes with the roast, if the children fall into the mud simultaneously with the advent of clean aprons, if the new girl quits in the middle of housecleaning, and though you search the earth with candles you find none to take her place, if the neighbor in whom you have trusted goes back on you and decides to keep chickens, if the chariot wheels of the uninvited guest draw near when you are out of provender, and the gaping of your empty purse is like the unfilled mouth of a young robin take courage if you have enough sunshine in your heart, to keep a laugh on your lips. Before good nature, half the cares of daily living will fly away like midges before the wind; try it.

XVII.

HOLD! ENOUGH!!

The other evening it chanced that a combination of disastrous circumstances wrought havoc with my temper. I lost my train; my head hummed like a bumblebee with weary pain, and the elastic that held my hat to its moorings broke, so that that capering compromise between inanimate matter and demoniac possession blew half a block up street on its own account, and was brought back to me by a youthful son of Belial, who took my very last quarter as reward for the lively chase.

"There's no use!" said I to myself as I jogged along through the gloaming; "blessed be the woman who knows enough to cry 'hold!' against such odds!"

And just then I spied a wizened little mite of a woman trotting by, carrying a gripsack bigger than herself. She grasped it, and held it against her wan little stomach, as a Roman warrior might carry his shield into battle—plucky to the last.

"Now," said I, "look here, Amber, have you a fifty pound sachel to tug through the darkness? No! Then you might be worse off."

And I went on a little farther and I met the brave firemen going home drenched and worn from the big fire. "You coward!" said I to myself, "what if you were a fireman! Something to growl about then, I guess."

And I went a bit farther and I saw a little white coffin in a window. "How about that?" said I. "If the darlings were gone to their long home you might talk about trouble!"

And a few moments later I ran across an old man without any legs, peddling papers. And then I said: "Do you call your life a grind, madam, with two legs to walk upon, and a sufficient income to admit of an occasional fling? What if you had wooden legs, and peddled papers?"

Now, I have told you this for a purpose. However dark your lot may be there are worse all around you. You may be inclined to think that the bloom and the brightness have gone out of your life, leaving nothing behind them but what remains of the carnation when the frost finds it—a withered stalk. But if you will take the trouble to watch, you will find that there is always something harder to bear than your own trouble, and, put to the test, you wouldn't change crosses with your neighbor.

XVIII.

RIPE OPPORTUNITIES.

What if a man went over the lake to St. Joe to visit the peach or-chards at the maturity of their delicious harvest! The consent of the owner of the fairest plantation of the many has been gained, let us imagine, for the plucking of the perfect fruit. And yet, in despite of opportunity and privilege, what would you think of one who came home with empty baskets and an unappeased relish for ripe peach-es? Would you not think such a one a dullard, or, at least, stupidly blind to his opportunities? And if you chanced to hear him crying over his empty basket later on, would you not revile him for a lazy fellow? We all of us, from day to day, miss chances of far greater value than the ripest peach that ever mellowed in the sun. The op-portunity to say a kind and encouraging word swings low upon the bough of to-day. Why not gather it in? The chance to help, to succor, to protect, the chance to lend a helping hand, to share a burden, to soothe a sorrow, to plant a loving thought, or twine a memory that shall blossom like a rose upon the terrace of to-morrow, all are our own as we pass through the world on our way to heaven. We may not come this way again. See to it, then, that we carry full baskets on the homeward faring.

XIX.

A SUNSET CLOUD.

Not long ago there slowly ascended into the evening sky a pillar of cloud so vast that all measurements sank into insignificance be-side it. Its color was of softest gray just touched with the flush that deepens the inmost chamber of a shell, or blushes in the unfolded petals of a wind flower. With majestic yet almost imperceptible motion this cloud mounted the blue background of the sky. The spectre of a faded moon hung motionless above it an instant only, and then was swiftly drawn within its soft eclipse. Changing from moment to moment, the great mass took on all semblances of vivid fancy, until the evening sky seemed the arena of dreamland's co-horts. With indescribable grace and with the delicate lightness of a fairy footfall the mighty visitant advanced and took possession of the heavenly field. Suddenly the full glory of the setting sun smote it from outer rim to base. In less time than it takes to tell the story the cloud was dissipated in a spray of feathery light. It drifted like a wreath before the wind and lost itself in the illimitable spaces of the air, as dust in the splendor of a summer day. It broke upon the hills in a shower of flame and dissolved above the still waters of the lake in tremulous flakes of light. The sight was worth going far to see, and yet I am willing to wager my to-morrow's dinner that not one-fiftieth of the folks for whom I write, saw it, or would have left their supper to watch the glorious spectacle.

XX.

ONE SECRET OF SUCCESS.

There is just one thing nowadays that never fails to bring success, and that is assurance. If you are going to make yourself known, it is no longer the thing to quietly hand out your card and a modest credential; you must advance with a trumpet and blow a brazen blast to shake the stars. The time has gone by when self-advancement can be gained by modest and unassuming methods. To stand with lifted hat and solicit a hearing savors of an all too humble spirit. The easily abashed may starve in a garret, or go die on the highways. There is no chance for them in the jostle of life. The gilded circus chariot, with a full brass band and a plump god-dess distributing posters, is what takes the popular heart by storm. Your silent entry into town, depending upon the merits of your wares to work up a trade, is chimerical and obsolete. We no longer sit in the shadow and play flutes; we parade in a sawdust ring and play on trombones, or take our place on a raised platform and beat the bass drum, and in that way we draw a crowd and gather in the coppers, and that is what we live for, isn't it?

XXI.

A NEW BEATITUDE.

There should be a new beatitude, and it should read, "Blessed is the man who hath the courage of his convictions." It should apply to poor, long-suffering women as well. We have plenty of the sort of courage that will lead a man to step in front of a runaway horse, or dash into a burning house, or throw himself off a dock to rescue a perishing wretch, but there is a dearth of the kind of bravery that will enable either man or woman to face a laugh in defense of a principle, or succor a losing cause despite a sneer. How the best of us will retreat trailing our banner in the dust, when the hot shot of ridicule confronts us from the enemy's camp, or when some merry sentinel challenges us with the opprobrious epithet, "crank." Why, I believe there is hardly a man or woman to-day who would have the courage to march up to a half-grown boy and knock the cigarette out of his mouth, or tackle the omnipresent, from everlasting to everlasting expectorator and buffet him into decency, or drive the "nose-bag" and the "head-check" fiend at the point of an umbrella from all future molestation of the noble horse he persecutes! We all believe in the extermination of public nuisances, but we have not the courage of our convictions to enable us to fight the fight of the just to overthrow the rampancy of the evil doer.

XXII.

BLESSED BE BASHFULNESS.

Like the presence of a fresh clover in a meadow of sun-scorched grasses, or the sound of a singing lark in a council of crows, is the sight of a bashful child. In this age of juvenile precocity and pinafore wisdom I would rather run across a downright timid boy or girl than drink Arctic soda in dog days. Never be distressed, then, when "johnnie" hangs his head and blushes like a girl, or when his little sister stands on one foot and fairly writhes with embarrassment in the presence of strangers. Count it rather the very crown of joy that you are the parent of a fresh and innocent child, rather than the superfluous attendant of a *blasé* infant, who discounts a circus herald in "cheek" and outdistances a drummer in politic address and unabashed effrontery. If I had my way I would put half the little mannikins and pattern dolls of our latter day nurseries into a big corn-popper and see if I couldn't evolve something sweeter and more wholesome out of the hard, round, compact little kernels of their present individuality. I would utterly do away with children's parties and "butterfly balls" and kirmess dissipations. There should be a new deal of bread and milk all around. Every boy in the land should go to bed at sundown, and every girl should wear a sun-bonnet. There should be no carrying of canes, or eating of candy, or wearing of jewelry, or talking of beaux, and I would dig up from the grave of the long ago the quaint old custom of courtesying to strangers, of keeping silent until spoken to, and of universal respect for the aged. This world would brighten up like a rose garden after a shower with the presence of so many modest little girls and bash-ful boys of the good old-fashioned sort.

XXIII.

A BEWITCHED VIOLIN.

I went to the Auditorium the other night to hear somebody play on the violin. But that was not a violin which the slender, dark eyed performer used, and the music that so charmed me was not drawn from strings and flashed forth by any ordinary bow. The heavenly notes to which I listened were like those that young leaves give forth when May winds find them, or that ripples make, drawn soft-ly over pebbly beaches. And when they died away and floated like a whisper through the hushed house, it was no longer music; it was a great golden-jacketed bee settling sleepily into the heart of a rose; it was the chime of a vesper-bell broken in mellow cadences be-tween vine-clad hills; it was a something that had no form nor shape, nor semblance to any earthly thing, yet floated midway be-tween the earth and sky, light as the frailest flower of snow the north wind ever cradled, substanceless as smoke or wind-followed mist.

XXIV.

A HAT PIN PROBLEM.

I overheard the following conversation the other day in a popular refectory:

"Do your children mind you?"

"I guess not; they never pay any more attention to me than if I was a dummy. It takes their father to bring them to terms every time!"

"I am so glad to hear it. I like to know that somebody else besides me has a hard time with their children. I declare the only way I can get baby to mind already is to jab him with a hat-pin!"

I waited to hear no more. With sad precipitation I gathered up my check and fled. Had I waited another minute I should have said to that mother: "Madam, I will give you a problem to solve. If, at the age of three, a child needs the impetus of one hat-pin to make him obey, how many meat-axes will it require to keep him in order at the age of ten? And if you are such a poor miserable failure as a mother and a woman now, just at the commencement of an immortal destiny, what have the eternities in store for you?"

Why, oh, why are children sent to people who have no more idea about bringing them up than a trout has about training hop-vines? It is a question that has given and does give me much uneasiness.

XXV.

POLITENESS VS. SINCERITY.

You imagine it is not polite to be plain spoken! My dear, there are times when to be merely "polite" is to be a toady! There are times when politeness is a pillow of hen feathers, wherewith to smother honor and strangle truth. If all you care for is to be popular, to go through life like a molasses-drop in a child's mouth, why, then, choose your way and live up to it, but don't expect to rank higher than molasses, and cheap molasses at that. For my part I would rather be outspoken in the cause of right, even if plain speech did offend, than be a coward and a woolly mouth. Somebody once lived upon earth, the example of whose thirty odd years of mortal environment we are taught to pattern our own lives close upon. How about his politeness when he talked with the hypocrites and rebuked the pharisees? How about his policy when he drove the money-changers before a stinging whip, and championed the cause of the sinful woman? Oh! I tell you, the soul that is always looking out for the chance to score one for the winning cause, and throw up its hat with the crowd that makes the most noise, is poor stock to invest in. In the time of need such a friend would turn out worse than a real estate investment in a Calumet swamp.

XXVI.

THE MOST DANGEROUS WOMAN.

Shall I tell you plainly, and without any mincing, what type of woman I think the most dangerous? It is not the virago, the wounds of a sharp tongue are hard enough to bear, but there is a balm for them. Mother may be overworked, or sister may be fretted; something is the matter with the digestion, often, when the one we love scolds and is excessively disagreeable in manner and speech. The harshest word is soon excused and overlooked by the smile and the caress that are sure to follow. So, bad as a scolding, nagging tongue may be, it has its alleviations, and somewhere there is an excuse made to fit it. But what palliation is there for the offense of the woman who seeks by blandishments and artifices of the evil one's own concoction to steal the affection of a man away from his wife? There are more such people in the world than you can imagine (and the evil is not confined to the one sex either.) An intriguing woman (or man) who steals into a happy home and seeks to undermine it, deserves to be stoned on the highway. She may steal your purse, your diamonds, or your checkbook, and, while love reigns on its rightful throne, the home will be happy; but let her seek to discrown love, and entertain a clandestine passion in its place, and the foundation of the stoutest home that was ever founded on the rocks of time will tumble in ruin about her ears. Avoid the intriguing, fascinating, dangerous, designing woman, then, who recognizes no sanctity in wedded honor, and by her wiles and witcheries lets in a thousand devils to the heart and home she curses with her presence.

XXVII.

SERMONS FROM FLIES.

I chanced to stand the other day in a stuffy little room, the only window of which was shaded by a ground glass light. Before the gray void of this cheerless window a few flies darted hither and thither in consequential flurry, while I myself, for the time being a most blue and down-cast mortal, was battling with the thought that life, after all, was hardly worth the living, and the outlook for anything better in a dim and uncertain future, too dubious to be entertained. But all at once my vision seemed to pierce the shaded pane that intervened between me and the great, rushing, riotous world, and such a conception of all that lay the other side the ground glass window overflowed my soul, that I felt rebuked as by an audible voice.

XXVIII.

THE MAN WHO KNOWS IT ALL.

There is a type of humanity we all encounter from day to day, at whose funeral I shall carry a banner and beat a tom-tom. He is the man who knows it all. In his grave, human forethought, and general knowledge, and mortal perfection and everything worth knowing, shall one day lie down and die. He never makes mistakes, nor loses his temper, nor gets the worst of an argument, nor is worsted in a bargain. He never acts on impulse, nor jumps without looking, nor commits himself rashly, nor loses the wind out of his sails. He is so overwhelmingly superior (sometimes he is a woman!) that in his presence you are a child of wrath, a hopeless imbecile, and a black sheep all in one, and yet—how you hate him and how you long to see some brave young David come along and hit him with a sling shot! Such a man as he, is fitted to bring the average human to the dust as quickly and as surely as a well aimed bullet brings down a wild duck.

XXIX.

BALD HEADS AND UNEQUAL CHANCES.

What a superior chance a man has in this world over a woman! In the matter of physical attributes alone his innings are as far ahead of hers as the man who carries the banner in a Fourth of July procession is ahead of the little boy who tugs along behind with the lemonade pail. The other evening I attended the theatre, and casting my eye over the audience between acts, I beheld no less than a score of bald-headed men. They were composed, and even cheerful, under an infliction that would have ostracized a woman. Imagine a man taking a bald-headed woman to see the "Railroad of Love!" Imagine a bald-headed girl with a fat, red neck and white eyelashes being in eager demand for parties, coaching jubilees or private suppers. There never was a man so homely, so halt, so deficient in beauty or brain that he could not get a wife when he wanted, but the candidates for the position of mistress of any man's household must be pretty, graceful and sweet. The chances are uneven, my dear, but what are you going to do about it?

XXX.

HUMAN STRAWS.

There is not much credit in being jolly when the joints of life are well oiled and events move as smoothly as feathers drawn through cream. The glory lies in maintaining your serenity under adverse circumstances; in emulating Mark Tapley, and being jolly when there is not a hand's breadth of blue in all the heavens. There are straws laid upon us every day, which, if they do not break our backs, at least go far to loosen the vertebrae of our temper. One of these straws is the man who expectorates in public places. What shall I do with that man? I cannot kill him, because there is a law against the violent removal of even a human straw. To be sure, he is the most insignificant straw that the wind of destiny blows across the waste of life. He never will mature a head of wheat though you give him eleven eternities to do it in. But he serves his purpose, and breaks the back of toleration.

XXXI.

A SALLOW FACED GIRL FOR YOUR PITY.

On the opposite corner sits a half-grown girl peddling apples. She polishes the fruit occasionally with a rag that she carries about her person (let us humbly hope it is not her handkerchief!) and now and then breaks into a double shuffle to dissipate the chill that invades her ill-clothed frame. What taste of joy do you suppose that child ever got out of the pewter cup the fates pour for her? Does she ever find time to run about with other children, playing the games which the generations hand down from one to the other? Does she ever play "tag," or "gray wolf," or "I spy?" Does she ever swing in a hammock like other girls when the days are long and blithe and sweet, as free from care as a cloud or a butterfly? Does life hold for her one sparkle in its poor cup of wine, one flavor that is not sordid and low and mean? You say it is easy to sit here all day selling apples, and wonder why I hold this sallow-faced girl up for special pity. To be sure there is no hardship in the part of her life visible to us. But in her dull soul lurks constantly the shadow of an ever present fear. The poor child is accountable to a cruel master, whether father or mother it matters little, who beats her each night that she returns to her wretched home with a scanty showing of nickels; and the consciousness of dull times and slow sales keeps her in a state of trepidation, which in you or me, my dear, would soon lapse into "nervous prostration," a big doctor's fee, and a change of air. Yet mark my words, if the dark-browed liberator of sorrow's captives were to proffer my little fruit peddler the exchange of death for all this wearing apprehension and constant toil, do you think she would accept the transfer? Not she. The "captain" out snow-balling to-day in her love-guarded home, with never a fear to shadow her sunny eyes, nor a big sorrow to start the showery tears, would not plead harder for the boon of longer living.

XXXII.

AND YET HE CLINGS TO LIFE.

As I sit here by my window I am reminded that this is a queer world and queer be the mortals that pass through it. There is that wreck of a man over yonder squeezing a bit of weird melody out of an old accordion and expecting the tortured public to throw a penny into his hat now and then to pay him for his trouble. Do you suppose that man knows what happiness means, as God designed it. He was, without doubt, a sad and grimy little baby once, brought up on gin slightly adulterated with his mother's milk. He was pounded daily before he was two years old, starved and cuffed and

kicked all the way up to manhood, and now his neck is so complete-
ly under the heel of hydra-headed disaster, wickedness and want,
that all he can find to do in this big and busy world is to sit on the
sidewalk and lacerate the public ear with those dreadful discords.
And yet, if death were to step up to that beggar's side and offer him
release, instant and sure, in the form of a falling brick or a horse
running amuck on the crowded sidewalk, he would cling to the
miserable shred he calls life as eagerly as though he were the crown
prince himself, with the heritage of his kingdom yet unwon.

XXXIII.

OH! TO RID THE WORLD OF SHAMS.

If you go to a florist and ask for a sweet pink root, you may get
fooled on the label, but when blooming time comes round there will
be no difficulty in deciding whether the flower you took on trust
was pink or onion. Plant a seed in the horticultural kingdom by any
name you please, there will be no mistake possible when June
comes. A carrot is bound to yield carrots, and a rose will repeat the
bright wonder of its beauty throughout the dreamy summer days,
in spite of any other name the florist may have blundered upon in
the labeling. Not so with humanity. There are souls that pass
through life with the label of lily, balm or heart's-ease tagged to
them, when they are nothing better than wild onion at heart. There
are lives sown in out of the way places, and carelessly passed by as
weeds, whose blossom angels might stoop to wear in the whiteness
of their own pure breasts. Oh, to rid the world of its shams! To
sweep away the "Chadbands" with a feather duster, as the new girl
removes dust; to open the windows and shoo away the traitors as
one drives flies, to hoe out society plats as one hoes garden beds,
and thin out the flaunting weeds so that the lilies may find room to
grow; to turn the strong light of discerning truth upon hypocrites
until, as the microscope changes a globule of dew into the abode of
10,000 wriggling abominations, so the deceitful heart shall stand
revealed for what it actually is, rather than for what it seems to be.

XXXIV.

DRESS PARADE OF THE GREAT ALIKE

I am tired of the endless dress parade of the "Great Alike." I am weary of walking in line, like convicts in stripes. I glory in cranks who serve their own individuality and are in bondage to nobody. The onward sweep of progress in this age has opened up the way for non-conformists. It is not a matter of heresy, nowadays, to think for yourself, dress for yourself, and be yourself. I confess that I have no heart pinings for such nonconformists as Dr. Mary Walker or any other individual who believes that eccentricity, serving no purpose but to make one conspicuous, is interesting. There are certain general rules of conduct that must be observed or the world would go to wreck like a wild freight train. It would be embarrassing to all concerned were I to decline to conform to the conventional custom of wearing shoes and bonnets, but when fashion ordains French heels and dead birds, if I decline to walk in file with the conformist, I am something of a hero, perhaps, and certainly preserve my own self-respect better than if I yielded to either a harmful or a cruel custom. When etiquette rules that I go through the world armed with a haughty reserve, like a picket soldier with a shotgun, if I conform to that rule, I act upon the warm impulses of natural living as the refrigerator acts upon meat; I may preserve the proprieties, but I chill the juices.

XXXV.

IF GOD MADE YOU A WILLOW DON'T TRY TO BE A PINE

I wish I could spend a fortnight in a world where folks dared to be true to themselves; where the conformist was shelved with last year's calendars, and a man studied out his own route to heaven and had the courage to walk in it. I would like to dwell with individuals and not with packs of human cards shuffled together in sets. I would like to feel my soul kindle into respect for distinct personalities, each one making his garment after his own measurement, and not trying to fit his coat after the cut of his neighbor's jacket. I would like to live for a while with men and women, rather than with human sheep blindly following a leader. Life is something better than a sheep-path aimlessly skirting the hills. It is a growth upward through the infinite blue into heaven. It is the spreading of many and various branches. If you are a willow, don't attempt to be a pine, and if the Lord made you to grow like an elm don't pattern yourself after a scrub oak. The rebuke "what will people say?" should never be applied to the waywardness of a child. Teach it rather to ask: "How will my own self-respect stand this test?" Such training will evolve something rarer in the way of development than a candle-mold or a yard-stick.

XXXVI.

TWO TYPES.

How full the streets are, to be sure! Where do all the folks come from and where do they stop? Surely there are not roofs enough to cover the steady stream of humanity that courses through the thoroughfares from dawn to night time. To one who walks much to and fro in the town there comes a rare chance to study human types. Books hold nothing within their covers so grotesque and so pathetic, so inexplicable and so queer as the folks that jostle one another on the streets! There is the precise female who nips along in a little apologetic way, as though there was an impropriety in the very act of locomotion for which she would fain atone. From the crown of her head to her boot tips she is proper, stupid and decorous, but too much of her company would prove to endurance what sultry weather proves to cream. In fact, I think if I were told I had to live with some of the women I meet on the streets, I would fall on my hat pin, as the old Romans did upon their swords, as the pleasanter alternative. There is nothing more charming than a bright woman, but she must be superior to her own environments and be able to talk and think about other things than a correct code of etiquette, her costumes and her domestic concerns.

There is a man I sometimes encounter on the street between whom and myself there looms a day of bitter reckoning. He wears rubbers if the day is at all moist, and next to ear muffs, galoshes on an able bodied man goad me to fury. If the Lord made you a man, be a man and not a molly-coddle. Soup without meat, bread without salt, pie-crust without a filling, slack-baked dough, all these are prototypes of the man without endurance or sufficient stamina to stand getting his delicate feet dashed with dew, or his shell-like ears nipped by frost.

XXXVII.

A DREAM GARDEN.

Country living is delightful, but, like all other blessings, it has its alternates of shadow. I used to sit here by my window last April and gloat over the prospects for the vegetable garden a tramp laid out and seeded for me in the early spring. What luscious peas were going to clamber over the trellis along about the middle of July! What golden squashes were going to nestle in the little hollows! What lusty corn was going to stride the hillocks! What colonies of beans and beds of lettuce should fill the spaces, like stars in the wake of a triumphant moon, and how odorous the breath of the healthful onion should be upon the midsummer air! But listen. No Assyrian ever yet came down upon the fold as my neighbor's chickens have descended upon the fair territory of my garden. As for shooing a chicken off, my dear, when its gigantic intellect is set upon scratching up a seeded bed, you might as well attempt to wave back a thunderstorm with a fan.

I have undertaken several difficult things in my life, but never one so hopeless as convincing a calm and resolute hen that she is an intruder. I spent one glad summer trying to keep a brood out of a geranium bed, and had typhoid fever all the fall just from overwork and worry. But say there had been no chickens to "wear the heart and waste the body," how about potato bugs, and caterpillars and huge and gruesome slugs? I never go out to sprinkle the sad pea vines or pick the drooping lettuce but what I resolve myself into a magnet to lure the early vegetable-devouring reptile from its lair. Large 7 by 9 caterpillars and zebra-striped ladybugs disport themselves on neck and ankle until I flee the scene.

XXXVIII.

ANYTHING WORSE THAN A BLUE-JAY? HARDLY!

If there is anything worse than a blue-jay, name it. Perhaps a mannish woman, with a shrill voice and a waspish tongue, is as bad, but she can't be worse. There are something less than a hundred of these feathered hornets dwelling in the grove that surrounds my house, and they began before sunrise to call names and fight clamorous battles. One of them starts the row by crying something in the ear of a neighbor, which sounds like a challenge blown through a fish horn. At this the insulted neighbor flops down off the tree where he lives, and says naughty words very thick and very fast. Then five or six old ladies poke their heads over the sides of their nests and call "Police!" A squad of bluecoats comes tearing ever the border and attacks the original culprit. He whips out his fish horn and summons a general uprising. Very soon there is a battle royal, to which the old ladies add zest by squeaking out dire threats in shrill falsetto voices pitched at high "C." This keeps up until somebody arises and declaims from my open window, dancing meanwhile in helpless rage, to see how futile is the voice of august man when blue-jays hold the floor. Talk about the English sparrow! It is a mild-mannered little gentleman compared to the noisy jay. Its politeness and amiability are Chesterfieldan beside the behavior of its handsomely attired but boorish neighbor. And as for fighting, why, I verily believe a bluejay in good condition could "do up" John L. Sullivan so quickly the gentle pugilist would never know what struck him.

XXXIX.

GOOD HEALTH A BLESSING.

What roses are with worms in the bud, such are women without health. There can be no beauty in unwholesomeness, there can be nothing attractive in a delicate pallor caused by the disregard of hygiene, or in a willowy figure, the result of lacing. If I could now and then thread some particular bead on an electric wire that should tingle and thrill wherever it touched, or write in a streak of zig-zag light across the sky, I might, perhaps, compel attention to what I have to say. There are certain laws of health which, if they only might be regarded, would make us all as beautiful in outward seeming as we strive to be, no doubt, in spirit. Ever so pure and lovely a soul in an unhealthy body is like a bird trying to thrive and sing in an ill-kept cage, or a flower blooming with a blight set deep within its withering petals. You or I can serve neither heaven nor mankind worthily if we disregard the laws of health, and bear about with us a frail and poorly nurtured body. There are "shut in" spirits, to be sure, captives from birth to pain, the record of whose patient endurance of suffering sweetens the world in which they live, as a rose shut within a dull and prosy book imparts to its pages a fragrance born of summer and heaven; but such lives are the exception. The true destiny of the sons and daughters of earth is to grow within the garden of life as a sapling rather than as a sickly weed, developing timber rather than pith, and yielding finally to death, the sharp-axed old woodman, as the tree falls, to pass onward to new opportunities of power and service. The tree does not decay where it stands, nor does it often fall because its core is honeycombed by disease. It is cut down in the meridian of its strength, because somewhere on distant seas a new ship is to be launched and needs a stalwart mainmast, or a home is to be builded that needs the fiber of strong and steadfast timber. So, I think, with men and women, there would not be so much unsightly growing old, with waning power and wasted faculties, if we attended more strictly to the laws of health, and when death came to us at last it should only be because there was need of good timber further on.

XL.

WHY, BLESS MY SOUL! IT REALLY SEEMS TO THINK.

I was watching not long since, a man talking to a bright woman on the train, and his manner of comporting himself set me to thinking of the peculiar ways men have of addressing themselves to women. Some talk to a woman very much as they might talk to the wonderful automaton around at the museum when it plays a game of chess. "Why, bless my soul, it really seems to be thinking! What apparent intelligence? What evident faculty of mental independence! It almost appears to possess the power of coherent thought!" Others sit in the presence of a woman as though she was a dish of ice cream. "How sweet." "How refreshing." "How altogether nice!" Many behave in her company as though she was a loaded gun, and liable to do mischief, while a very few act as though she was above the wiles of flattery, and not to be bought for the price of a new bonnet. Hasten the day, good Lord, when she shall be regarded as something wiser and nobler than an automaton, less perishable than a confection, more comforting and peace-producing than a fire-arm, a veritable comrade for man at his best, not so much prized for the vain and evanescent charm of her beauty as for the steadfastness and the incorruptible purity of her soul.

XLI.

TAKE TO DRINK, OF COURSE!

What would a man do, I yonder, if things went so irretrievably wrong with him as they do with some of us women? Why, take to drink, of course. That is a sovereign consolation I am told for many ills. A woman has no equivalent for whisky. She must needs clench her hands and set her teeth and bear her lot. And yet you tell us a man is the stronger. I tell you, my dear, I know a dozen women who could discount any soldier that ever fought in the Crimean wars, for downright heroism and pluck. Where do you find the man who is willing to wear shabby clothes and old boots and a seedy hat that his boys may go fine as fiddles? Where do you find a man who will get up cold mornings and make the fire, tramp to work through snow, pick his way through flooding rain, weather northeast blasts and go hungry and cold that he may keep the children together which a bad and wayward mother has deserted? First thing a man would do in such a case would be to board the children out with convenient relatives while he looked around for a divorce and another wife! How long would a man brace up under the servant question? How long would he endure the insolence and the flings of cruel and covert enemies because the children needed all he could give them, and, only along the thorny road of continual harassment and trial might he attain the earnings needed to render them happy and comfortable? If a man is insulted he settles the insult with a blow straight from the shoulder and that is the end of it; he would never be able to endure, as some women do, a never-ending round of persecution that would whiten the hairs on a sealskin jacket!

XLII.

A WARNING TO GIRLS.

There is one thing we sometimes see in the face of the young that is sadder than the ravages of any disease or the disfigurement of any deformity. Shall I tell you what it is? It is the mark that an impure thought or an unclean jest leaves behind it. No serpent ever went gliding through the grass and left the trail of defilement more palpably in its wake than vulgarity marks the face. You may be ever so secret in your enjoyment of a shady story, you may hide ever so cunningly the fact that you carry something in your pocket which you purpose to show only to a few and which will perhaps start the laugh that, like a bird of carrion, waits upon impurity and moral corruption for its choicest feeding, but the mark of what you tell, and what you do, and what you laugh at, is left behind like a sketch traced in indelible fluid. There is no beauty that can stand the disfigurement of such a scar. However bright your eyes, and rosy-red your color, and soft the contour of lip and cheek, when the relish of an impure jest creeps in, the comeliness fades and perishes, as lilies in the languor of a poisonous breath from off the marshes. I beg of you, dear girls, shun the companion who seeks to foul your soul with an obscene story or picture, as you would shun the contagion of smallpox. If I had a daughter who went out into the world to earn her bread, as some of you do, and any one should seek to corrupt her purity by insidious advances, I would get down on my knees and pray God, to take her to himself before her fair, sweet innocence should sully under the breath of corruption and moral death. Nobody ever went to the devil yet by one big bound, like a tiger out of a jungle or a trout to the fly; it is an imperceptible passage down an easy slope, and the first step of all is sometimes taken when a young girl lends her ears to a smutty story or a questionable jest. Then let me say again, and I wish I could borrow Fort Sheridan's bugle to blow it far and wide, that every girl might hear: Close your ears and harden your hearts against the insidious advance of evil. Have nothing to do with a desk-mate or with a comrade who seeks to amuse or entertain you with conversation you would not care to have "mother" hear, and which you would be sorry to remember, if this night the death angel came knocking at the door and summoned your soul away upon its lonely journey to find its God.

XLIII.

A FROG MAY DO WHAT A MAN MAY NOT.

A bull-frog in a malarial pond is expected to croak and make all the protest he can against his surroundings. But a man! Destined for a crown and sent upon earth to be educated for the court of the King of kings! Placed in an emerald world with a hither edge of opaline shadow and a fine spray of diamond-dust to set it sparkling; with ten million singing birds to form its orchestra; sunset clouds and sunrise mists to drape it, and countless flowers to make it sweet while the hand of God himself upholds it on its way among the clustering stars, what right has a man to find fault with his surroundings, or lament himself that all things do not go to suit him here below? When it shall be in order for the glow-worm to call the midday sun to account, or for the wood-tick to find fault with the century old oak that protects it; or for the blue-bird to question the haze on a midsummer horizon because, forsooth! it is a little off color with his own wings, then it will be time for man to find fault with the ordering of the seasons and the allotment of the weather in the world he is allowed to inhabit.

XLIV.

THANKING GOD FOR A GOOD HUSBAND.

About one hour of the twenty-four would perhaps be the proportion of time a woman ought to spend upon her knees thanking God for a good husband. When I see the hosts of sorry maids, and women wearing draggled widow's weeds who fill the ranks of the great army of the self-supporting; when I see them trooping along in the rain, slipping along in the mud, leaping for turning bridges, and hanging on to the straps in horse cars, I feel like sending out a circular to sheltered and happy wives bidding them be thankful for their lot. To be sure, one would rather be a scrub-woman or a circus-jumper than be the wife of some men we wot of, but in the main, a woman well married is like a jewel well set, or like a light well sheltered from the wind.

XLV.

JUST A LITTLE TIRED!

What a grubby old stopping place this world is, anyway. How hard we have to work just to keep the flesh on our bones and that flesh covered, even with nothing better than homespun. And we are getting a little tired of it all, aren't we, my dear? Just a little tired of the treadmill, where, like a sheep in a dairy, we pace our limited beat to bring a handful of inadequate butter. We have trudged to and fro about long enough, and have half a mind to throw up the contract with fate. But hold on a bit. There is something worse than too much work, and that is idleness. Imagine a sudden hush in all the myriad sounds of labor. The ceasing of the whirr of countless wheels whereat men stand day after day through toilful years, fashioning everything from a pin's head to a ship's mast; the suspended click of millions of sewing machines, above which bend delicate women stitching their lives into shirts and garments that find their way onto bargain tables, where rich women crowd to seize the advantage of the discount. Let all suspended hammers in the myriad workshops swing into silence and all footsteps cease their weary plodding to and fro, I think the awful hush would far transcend the muteness of midnight or that still hour when dawn steals in among the pallid stars, and on the dim, uncertain shore of time the tide of man's vitality ebbs faint and low. There is no blight so fell as the blight of enforced calm. It is in the unworked garden that weeds grow. It is in the stagnant water that disease germs waken to horrid life. Ennui palls upon a brave heart. Ennui is like a long-winded, amiable, but watery-idea'd friend who drops in to see us and dribbles platitudes until every nerve is tapped. Ennui is like being forced to drink tepid water or to eat soup without salt. Labor, on the contrary, is like a friend with grit and tonic in his make-up. It comes to us as a wind visits the forest, and sets our faculties stirring as the wind rustles the leaves and sets the wood fragrance flying. It puts spice in our broth and ice in our drink. It puts a flavor in life that starts an appetite, or, in other words, awakens ambition. Although the world is full of toilers it would be worse off were it full of idlers. Good, hard workers find no time to make mischief. Your anarchists and your breeders of discord are never found among busy men; they breed, like mosquitoes, out of stagnant places. It is the idle man that quickens hatred and contention, as it is the setting hen and not the scratching one that hatches out the eggs.

XLVI.

PAINTING THE OLD HOMESTEAD.

It had been a battle renewed for more years than there are dandelions just now in the front yard. Various members of the family had declared from time to time that if the old house was not painted it would fall to pieces from sheer mortification at its own disreputable appearance.

"Why, you can put your toothpick right through the rotten shingles," cried the doctor. "The only way to save it is to paint it."

Now, I have always been the odd sheep of a highly decorous fold. I have more love for nature than hard good sense, I am told. So I loathe paint just as I hate surface manners. I want the true grain all the way through, be it in boards or people. I love the weather stain on an old house. I love the mossy touches, the lichen grays and the russet browns that age imparts to the shingles, and I almost feel like murdering the paint fiend when he comes around every spring, and transforms some dear old landmark into a gorgeous "Mrs. Skewton," with hideous coats and splashy trimmings. But alas for sentiment when the money bags are against it! Profit before poetry any day in this nineteenth century, my dear, and so when an interested capitalist came up from town and gave it as his opinion that the old house would be worth a third more if put on the market in a terra cotta coat with sage-green trimmings the day was lost for me. I had to strike my colors like many another idealist in this practical world. In the first place, there has been for the last fifteen years or so, a vine growing all over the old home, catching its lithe tendrils into the roof and making cathedral lights in all the windows. It has been the home of generations of robins. It has hung full of purple, bell-shaped blossoms on coral stems that have attracted a thousand humming birds and honey bees by their fragrance. It has changed into a veritable cloth of gold in early September, and in late October has flamed into scarlet against the gray roof, like a blaze that quivers athwart a stormy sky. It has been the joy of my life and the inspiration of my dreams, but it had to come down before the paintpot! So one night when I reached home, tired to death with a hand-to-hand encounter with the demon who gives poor mortals their bread and butter for an equivalent of flesh and blood and spirit, I noticed that the little folks greeted me with an air of subdued decorum as though fresh from a funeral. There were no caperings, no flauntings, no cavortings. Each young minx had on her Sunday go-to-meeting air, and the boy stood with his hat on one side of his head, as though for a sixpence he would fight all creation. Wondering at the change, I happened to look toward the house, and there it stood in the light of the fading day, like a poor old woman without a veil to hide her wrinkles! Every window looked ashamed of itself, and on the ground lay the dear old vine, prone as a lost reputation.

"I never see such an ill-fired crank in all the days of my life!" remarked the painter to the new girl, after I had held a brief but spirited interview with him over the garden fence; "blanked if she didn't cry because her vine was down!"

XLVII.

THE OLD SITTING-ROOM STOVE.

What is there within the home, during the winter season at least, that seems so thoroughly to constitute the soul of home as the family-room stove? It can never be replaced by that ugly hole in the floor which floods our rooms with furnace heat, with no glow of cheerful firelight, no flicker of flame or changeful play of shadow out of which to weave fantastic dreams and fancies. I once watched the dying out of one of these fires in a great base burner, around which for years a large and loving family had gathered. The furniture of the home had all been sold, and the family was about to scatter. The trunks were packed and gone, the last article removed from the place, and the old stove was left to burn out its fire at the last, that it, too, might be removed next morning. And after the evening had come and was far spent, the last evening wherein any right should remain to us to enter the old home as its owners and occupants, I took my pass-key and slipped over from the neighbor's for my final good-bye to the dear old home. The fire-light, like the glance of a reproachful eye, shone upon me through the gloom of the deserted parlor. "Have I not warmed you and comforted you and cheered you with my genial glow?" a voice seemed to say; "and now you have come to see me die! I am the vital spirit of your home. I am dying, and nothing can ever reanimate these deserted rooms again with the dear, the beautiful past."

Like the eye of one who is going down to death, the firelight faded and finally went out in the pallor of ashes, while I, sitting alone in the darkness, felt the whole world drearier for a little space for the final extinguishment of this fire, the death hour of a once happy home.

XLVIII.

A TALK ABOUT DIVORCE.

Somebody asked me the other day if I favored divorce. Like everything else in the world the matter depends largely upon special circumstance, but in the main I do not believe in divorce. If husbands and wives cannot live together without quarreling, let them live apart, but they have no business to sever the bond that unites them. The promise to take each other for "better or for worse" must be regarded in both readings of the clause. If the "worse" comes along we have no right to ignore it because the "better" has failed. If your husband is a drunkard, all the more reason for you to stand by him if you are a good woman. If he is cruel and abusive, you need not put your life in danger by staying under his roof, but you need not throw him over and get another husband. If he goes into the gutter, pull him out, and know that your experience is only a big dose of the "worse" you promised to take along with the "better." It is the quinine with the honey, and you have no right to reject it. There are 10,000 things that work discord in married life that a little tact and forbearance would dissipate, as a steady wind will blow away gnats. The trouble with all of us is, we make too much of trifles. We nurse them, and feed them, and magnify them, until from gnats they grow to be buzzards with their beaks in our hearts. Not for one sin, nor seven sins, nor seventy sins, forsake the friend you chose from all the world to make your own. A good woman will save anything but a liar, and God's grace is adequate, in time, for even him. I say unto wives, be large-hearted, wide in your charity, generous, not paltry, nor exacting, (exaction has murdered more loves than Herod murdered babies!) companionable, forbearing and true, and stand by your husbands through everything. And I say unto men, be *men*! Don't choose a wife, in the first place, for the mere exterior of a pretty face and form. Be as alert in the choice of a wife as you are in a bargain. You don't invest in a house just because it looks well, or buy a suit of clothes at first sight, or dash on change and snatch at the first deal. After you are once married stand by your choice like a man. If you must have your beer, don't sneak out of it on a clove and a lie; carefully weigh the cost, and if you conclude to risk everything for the gratification of an appetite drink at home and above board, and don't attempt to deceive your wife with subterfuges and excuses. Don't run after other women because your wife is not so young as she once was, or because the bloom is faded a little from the face you once thought so fair. It is the part of an Indian to retract a gift once given, or to go back on a bargain. Don't live together if you can't rise above the level of fighting cats, but be careful how you throw aside the bonds that God has joined between you. Live the lot you have chosen as bravely as you can, remembering that the thorn that you have developed will never change into a rose by mere change of circumstances. Divorce and the mere shifting of the stage setting will never make your tragedy over into a vaudeville or a light opera.

XLIX.

GONE BACK TO FLIPPITY-FLOPPITY SKIRTS.

The rainy season is here again, and where is dress-reform? My soul grew sick, the other morning as, with unfurled umbrella, lunch-basket, bundle, and draperies, I beheld the working woman on her weary march. Give a man a petticoat, a bundle and an umbrella, and the streets would be full of capering lunatics whenever it rained. Stay at home, did you say? That is good advice for the woman who has nothing else to do, but in these latter days the right sort of husband don't go round. Either he died in the war or the stock has run low, so that more than half the well-meaning women have no homes to stay in. What Moses is going to lead the poor creatures to the commonsense suit that shall protect them from the inclement weather they are forced to meet as they go abroad to earn their bread and salt? It must be a concerted movement, for there is none among us who dares take the war path alone. The children of Israel went in a crowd and so must we. For a principle there are those among us who would die, perhaps, but there is no principle on the earth below nor in the heaven above for which we would suffer ridicule. As for me, I have furled my banner and laid aside my bugle. I am tired of being a martyr to an unpopular cause. I am too big a coward to be caught making an everlasting object of my-self. I have gone back to flippity-floppity skirts and long gowns and all the rest of the "flesh pots." Browning says of a certain class of people: "The dread of shame has made them tame," and I am one of the tame ones. A domestic tabby couldn't be tamer, nor a yellow bird fed on lump sugar. I expect nothing but that my winter's hat will be adorned with a chubby green parrot, and that I shall walk the street leading a brimstone dog by a magenta ribbon. If one is forced to eat, drink and sleep with the Romans, perhaps it is better for one's peace of mind not to be too pronounced a Greek!

L.

I SHALL MEET HIM SOME DAY.

I shall meet the man who ties his horse's nose in a bag, some day, in single combat, and there will be only one of us left to tell the tale of the encounter. Wouldn't I love to see that man forced to take his dinner while tied up in a flour bag! I should love to deal out his coffee through a garden hose, and serve his vegetables through a long-distance telephone. There is nothing like turn about to incite justice in the human breast. While we are afflicted with such an epidemic of strikes, why not have one that has some sense in it. Let the overworked horses, straining themselves blind with terrible loads, go on a strike. Let the persecuted dogs, deprived of water and scrimped for food, stoned and hounded as mad when they are only crazed by man's inhumanity, go on a strike. Let the cattle, and the countless thousands of stock, prodded into cars and cramped in long passages of transit, blinded with the crash of fellow-victims' horns while crowded together in their inadequate quarters, trampled under riotous hoofs, and kept without food and overfilled with water to make them look fat, go on a strike. Let the chickens and geese and all the live feathered stock on South Water Street, kept in little bits of coops and flung headlong and screaming down into dark cellars, trundled over rough roads in jolting wagons and utterly deprived for hours at a time of a drop of water to cool the fever of their terrible fear, go on a strike. Let the horses of these fat aldermen, left all day in the court house alleyway without food and checked tight with head-check lines, go on a strike. Let the patient nags that stand all day by the curbstone and are plagued and annoyed by mischievous boys, go on a strike. In such a strike as any of these the Lord himself might condescend to take sides with the oppressed against the oppressor.

LI.

A MANNISH WOMAN.

There are many disagreeable things to be met with in life, but none that is much harder upon the nerves than a mannish woman. With a strident voice and a swaggering walk, and a clattering tongue, she takes her course through the world like a cat-bird through an orchard; the thrushes and the robins are driven right and left before the advance of the noisy nuisance. A coarse-tongued man is bad enough, heaven knows, but when a woman descends to slangy speech, and vulgar jests, and harsh diatribes, there is no language strong enough with which to denounce her. On the principle that a strawberry is quicker to spoil than a pumpkin, it takes less to render a woman obnoxious than to make a man unfit for decent company. I am no lover of butter-mouthed girls, of prudes and "prunes and prism" fine ladies; I love sprightliness and gay spirits and unconventionality, but the moment a woman steps over the border land that separates delicacy of feeling, womanliness and lovableness, from rudeness, loud-voiced slang and the unblushing desire for notoriety, she becomes, in the eyes of all whose opinion is worth having, a miserable caricature upon her sex. It is not quite so bad to see a young girl making a fool of herself as to see an elderly woman comporting herself in a giddy manner in public places. We look for feather-heads among juveniles, but surely the cares and troubles of fifty years should tame down the high spirits of any woman. Chance took me into a public office the other day, largely conducted by women. Conspicuous among the clerks was a woman whose age must have exceeded fifty years. She was exchanging loud pleasantries with a couple of beardless boys upon the question of "getting tight." Noble theme for a woman old enough to be their grandmother to choose! As I listened to the coarse jests and looked into her hard and unlovely face, I could but wonder how nature ever made the mistake to label such material—"woman." It would be no more of a surprise to find a confectioner's stock made up of coarse salt, marked "sugar," or to buy burdock of a florist, merely because the tag attached to it was lettered "moss rose."

LII.

THE ONLY WAY TO CONQUER A HARD DESTINY.

The only way to conquer a cast-iron destiny is to yield to it. You will break to pieces if you are always casting yourself upon the rocks. Sit down on the "sorrowing stone" now and then, but don't expect to last long if you are constantly flinging yourself head first against it. If life holds nothing nobler and sweeter than the routine of uncongenial work, if all the pleasant anticipations and lively hopes of youth remain but as cotton fabrics do when the colors have washed away, if good intention and noble purpose glimmer only a little now and then from out the murky environments of your lot, as fisher lights at sea, accept the inevitable and make the best of it. Nothing can stop us if we are bound to grow. We are not like trees that can be hewed down by every chance woodman's axe; death is the only woodman abroad for us, and he does not hew down, he simply transplants. God is our only judge; to him alone shall we yield the record of life's troubled day, and isn't it a great comfort to think that he so fully understands what have been our limitations, and how we have been handicapped and baffled and hindered? If jockeys were to enter their horses for the great Derby with the understanding that the road was rough and the horses blind, do you think much would be expected of the finish? And is heaven less discriminating than a horse jockey?

LIII.

THE "SMART" PERSON.

Next to a steam calliope preserve me from a "smart" person. There is as much difference between smartness and brain as there is between a jewsharp and a flute, or between mustard and wine. A "smart" person may turn off a lot of work and make things hum, so does a buzz-saw! Who would not rather spend an afternoon with a lark than with a hornet? The lark may not be so active, but activity is not always the most desirable thing in the world. A smart person may accomplish more than a dreamer, but in the long run I'll take my chance with the latter. When we go up to St. Peter's gate by and by, after life's long, blundering march is over, it will not be the answer to such questions as this: "How many socks can you darn in an afternoon, besides baking bread, washing windows, tending babies and scrubbing floors?" that is going to help us; but, "How many times have you stopped your work to bind up a broken heart, or say a comforting word, or help carry a burden for somebody worse off than yourself?" I tell you, smart folks never have the time to be sympathetic; they always have too much thundering work on hand.

LIV.

A PRETTY STREET INCIDENT.

The other day a horse was trying to get a very small quantity of oats from the depths of a very small nosebag. In vain the poor fellow tossed his head and did his best to gain his dinner. At last, just as he was settling down to dumb and despairing patience, a bright-faced boy of perhaps ten or twelve years of age happened along. Seeing the dilemma of the horse, the little fellow stopped and said: "Halloa, can't get your oats, can you? Never mind, I'll fix you!" And straightway he shortened up the straps that held the bag in place, and, with a kindly pat and a cheery word which the grateful horse seemed to appreciate, went his way. I would like to be the mother, or the aunt, or even the first cousin of that boy. I would rather that he should belong to me than that I should own a Paganini violin, or a first-water diamond the size of a Concord grape. Bless his heart, wherever he is, and may he long continue to live in a world that needs him. Kindness of heart, and tenderness; consideration for the needs of the helpless and the weak, and the courage that dares be true to a merciful impulse, are traits that go far toward the make-up of angels. We need tender-hearted boys more than we need a new tariff to bring up and develop the resources of the country. The boy that succeeds in bringing in the greatest number of dead sparrows may be the embryo man of the future, and you may praise his energy and his smartness, but give me the boy who took the trouble to adjust the nose-bag every time. A little less business acumen, a good bit less greed and cruelty, will tell on future character to the comfort of all concerned.

LV.

POLICY A DAMASCUS BLADE, NOT A CLUB.

Policy in the hands of a diplomat is like a sharp sword in the grasp of an able fencer, but policy in the hands of fools, is like a good knife wielded by a half-wit. It takes brains to be truly politic, the unfortunate person who attempts to be cautious, and wise, and reticent, and to let policy thread every action as a string runs through glass beads, only succeeds in making himself ridiculous. To be afraid to speak what is in your mind for fear you will make yourself unpopular, to be too cautious to mention the fact that you are having a new latch put on your front gate for fear that you might be over-communicative, to be backward in taking sides for fear of committing yourself to a losing cause, may be politic to your own feeble intelligence, but in the estimation of brainy folks it is a species of feline idiocy worse than fits.

LVI.

THE CONSTANT YEARS BRING AGE TO ALL.

All day long it has been trying to snow out here in the country. To me not even June, with its showering apple-tree flowers and its alternations of silver rain and golden sunshine, is more beautiful than these soft winter days, full of snow-feathers and great shadows. I love to watch the young pines take on their holiday attire. How they robe themselves from head to foot in draperies of fleecy white, pin diamonds in their dark branches and wind about their slender girth the strands of evanescent pearl! I love to watch the skies at dawn when they kindle like a flame above the bluffs and scatter sparkles of light as a red rose scatters its petals. Where has the last year fled? It seems but yesterday that I sat by this same window and hatched the lilac plumes unfold on that old bush that to-day is getting ready to don its ermine. Why, at this rate, my dear, it won't be longer than day after to-morrow morning before you and I wake up and find ourselves old folks. How odd it will seem to look in the glass and see wisps of frosted stubble in place of the wavy locks of brown, and jet, and gold! Ah, well, it is a comfort to think that some folks defy time, and are as young at seventy as at seventeen. Beauty fades, and witchery takes unto itself wings, but true hearts, like wine, mellow and enrich with years.

LVII.

DID YOU EVER READ THE "LITTLE PILGRIM."

I often sit for a half hour or more in the depot waiting-room, and for lack of anything else to do employ the time in watching the people who crowd through the swinging doors. Did you ever read the "Little Pilgrim?" Do you recall the chapter wherein the disembodied spirits are represented as lingering near the gates to watch the coming in of newly liberated souls? Sometimes while sitting in one of the big rocking chairs I imagine to myself that the constantly opening doors are the portals of death and I the lingering one who watches the throngs that are constantly exchanging earth for paradise. Along comes an old man with a shabby bundle; he cautiously opens the door and slips in like one who offers an excuse for his presence on the thither side. Presently he lays down his bundle and seats himself, a pilgrim whose wanderings and weariness are over. The brilliant lights, the comfortable surroundings, the sound of pleasant voices all fill his heart with joy, and he settles himself back, thoroughly glad to be at rest. Next, a beautiful woman enters, her face is lined with care and her dark, bright eyes are full of trouble. She does not tarry, but hurries on like one seeking for something yet to come. A little child, with lingering, backward glance, flits through the swinging door as if loath to say good-bye to some one on the other side. A hard-featured man, whose sullen glance travels quickly about the place, comes next; he seems seeking for some one to welcome him, and is abashed to find himself alone among unheeding strangers. Next a bevy of laughing girls come in together, and the door, swinging quickly behind them, discloses a band of young companions who lingeringly turn away, content to know the sheltered ones are safely gathered out of the darkness and the storm which they must still face. Some enter the door as though bewildered; some as though glad to find rest; some as though frightened at unknown harm, and some as though suspicious of all that they beheld. Once I noticed a poor creature who came through the door crying bitterly, but her tears were quickly dried by a waiting one who sprang forward and greeted her with a tender embrace. And at another time a baby came through in the arms of one who held it close so that it was not conscious of the transition. Sometimes I am glad to believe that death is no more than the swinging door which divides two apartments in a mighty mansion, and that our going through is no more than the exchange of a cold and unlighted hallway for a spacious living-room where all is light and warmth and blessed activity.

LVIII.

EATING MILK TOAST WITH A SPOON!

Eating milk toast with a spoon and stopping between each mouthful to swear! That was what I saw and heard a brawny man doing not long since in a popular down-town restaurant. The action and the manner of speech did not harmonize. If I felt it borne in upon me that I must be a profane fellow to prove my manliness, I would choose another diet than spoon victuals to nourish my formidable zest for naughtiness. Rare beef or wild game would be less incongruous. There are times when a man may be excused for using objectionable language. Stress of righteous indignation, seasons of personal conflict with hansom cabmen, large-headed street car conductors, ubiquitous, never-dying expectorators and many other particular forms of torment may make a man swear a bit now and then, but what shall we say of a bearded creature with the dew of a babe's food upon his chin who rends the placid air with unnecessary cursing? Sew up his lips with a surgeon's needle and throw him into the fool-killer's bag!

LIX.

BOYS, YOU KNOW I LIKE YOU.

Boys, you know I like you and will stand a good deal of your swaggering ways. I like to see how fresh you are, and do not want to have you salted down too early by the processes of life. But one thing let me ask you. Don't wear silk hats before the down is fully apparent upon your chin. If there is an embarrassing sight left to one grown wan and worn in watching the foolishness of folly, it is the sight of a stripling in a plug hat. I would rather see a yearling colt hauling lumber, or a babe in arms scanning Homer. It is cruel; it is premature. Be a boy until you are fit to be a man, and hold to a boy's mode of dress at least until you are old enough to command the respect of sensible girls by something more notable than cigarette smoking and athletic sports.

LX.

WHAT TO DO WITH GROWLERS.

I often hear people making a big fuss about little things. My path in life leads me among many "kickers" and many "growlers." Do you know what I would like to do with some of these malcontents and whiners? I would like to send them up for a week to watch life in the county hospital. I would like to seat them by a bedside where a noble woman lies dying all alone of a terrible disease. I would like to have them become acquainted with her bravery and the more than queenly calm with which she confronts her destiny. I would like to have them linger in the corridors and hear the moans from the wards and private rooms where the maimed and the crippled and the incurable are faintly struggling in the grasp of death. I would like to lead them through the children's ward, where mites of humanity cursed with heredity's blight, removed from a mother's bosom, consigned to suffering throughout the span of their feeble days, lie faintly breathing their lives away. And then would like to say to them: "You contemptible cowards, you abominable fussers, you inexcusable kickers, see what the Lord might bring you to if he unloosed the leash and set real troubles in your track. Quit complaining and go to thanking heaven for all your unspeakable mercies!"

LXI.

GOD BLESS 'EM!

Every morning just at 7 the entire neighborhood turns out to see them pass. She is a demure little lady with a face that makes one think of a blush rose, a little past its prime, but mighty sweet to look upon. She wears a mite of a white sun-bonnet, clean as fresh fallen snow, and starched and stiff as the best pearl gloss cap make it. The cape of this cute little bonnet shades a round white throat, and the strings are tied beneath the chin in a ravishing bow that stands guard over a dimple. She has been married quite ten years, and they say that the two little children who were cradled for a few happy months on her soft breast are waiting and watching for her coming the other side of the river of death. He is a matter-of-fact looking man, with a resolute face and a constant smile in his eyes. He always carries a lunch-basket in one hand and with the other guides the steps of the faithful little woman who accompanies him part way on the march of his daily grind. He works downtown in a big warehouse and he makes hardly enough money each week to keep you in cigars, my good friend, or your wife in novels. Though it rain, or though it shine, though the winds blow or the winds are low, whatever betide of chance, or change, or weather, there is not a morning that he goes to work that she does not walk with him as far as the corner, and in the face of men and angels, grip car conductors and clerks, shop girls and grimacing urchins, kiss him good-bye. She stands and watches until he is well on his way, then waves him a final farewell, and trips back home in the serene shadow of her little bonnet. Now you may ridicule that love and call it "spoony" and "silly," but, I tell you, a legacy of gold or a hatful of diamonds could not begin to outvalue such love in a man's home. God bless the two, say I, and roll round the joyful day when love and its free and beautiful demonstration shall shine athwart the heresies of conventionality as April suns dispel the winter's fog with the splendor of their broadcast shining.

LXII.

"UNTO ONE OF THE LEAST OF THESE."

I was riding up-town in a cable car not long ago late at night. The moon was at its full and all the ugliness of the city was shrouded, like a homely woman in a bridal veil of shimmering lace. We skimmed along on a smooth and unobstructed track, like a sloop with every sail set, heading for the open sea. There were no idle chatterers aboard, and from the stalwart gripman at his post of duty, to the shrinking little girl passenger, who was half afraid and half delighted to be abroad so late alone, everybody and everything was in harmony with the hour and scene. Suddenly there fluttered into the car a snowy moth, astray from some flower garden in the country and quite bewildered and lost in the barren city. The beautiful creature fluttered into a lady's face and she screamed and struggled as though attacked by a rabid beast. "Oh, kill it! kill the horrid thing," she cried, while her attendant beat the air with his cane and sought to drive the dangerous interloper away. It rested for a moment upon the gripman's cap, where it looked like a feather dropped from a wandering bird. At last it settled upon the breast of a little child sleeping in its mother's arms. The mother brushed it away with her handkerchief as though its presence brought defilement. A gentleman who was seated near me caught the bewildered thing and with a very tender touch held it for a block or so until we came to one of the pretty parks that make our city so attractive. Stepping from the car, he loosened his grasp upon the captive moth near a big syringa bush that adorned the entrance way. He watched the dainty white wings flutter down into the cool seclusion of the blossom then turned and boarded the car and pursued his homeward way conscious, let us hope, of a very pretty and graceful deed of kindness to a most insignificant claimant for protection and succor. Sentimental, was it? Well, God help the world when all sentimentality of this kind is gone out of it.

LXIII.

TAKING INVENTORY.

How poor the most of us prove to be when we take inventory of the soul's stock! We have lots of bonnets, and plenty of dresses, and no end of lingerie, we women, but how are we off for the things that count when the dry goods and the furbelows shall be forgotten? How about love, of the right kind, the love that ennobles rather than degrades, and how about loyalty, and patience, and truth? If one of Chicago's big firms should close its doors to take inventory of stock in January and find it had nothing but the labels on empty bales to account for, its poverty would be as nothing to the poverty of the soul we are going to schedule shortly behind the closed door of the grave. What slaves we are to passion; how we hate one another for fancied or even actual slights, when we have such a little moment of time in which to indulge the evil tempers! How we bicker, and lie, and betray, the while the messenger stands already at the door to bid us begone from the scene of our petty conflicts. For my part, the interest we take in things that pertain to this perishable life, when we are so soon going where these are not to be; the choice we make of ranks and reputations, shams and seemings, dinners and wines, jewels and fabrics; the importance we attach to bubbles that break before we reach them; the allurements that draw us far from the ideals we started out to gain; the way we content ourselves with the environments of evil and forego forever the voice that calls us away to partake of things which shall be as wine and honey to the soul, frightens me; startles me as the sudden thunder of the surf might startle one who sojourned by an unseen sea.

LXIV.

DON'T MARRY HIM TO SAVE HIM.

If any young woman who reads this is contemplating marriage with a wild and wayward man, hoping to reform him, I want her to stop right here and decide to give up the contract. As well might she go out and smile down a northwest wind or expostulate with a cyclone to its own undoing. If a man drinks to excess before he marries, there is no reason to hope he will learn moderation afterward. If you become his wife with the full knowledge of his habits, you will have no right to leave him or forsake him after marriage because of his unfortunate addictions and predilections. Once having taken the vows you have no right to refuse to pay them to the uttermost. And the life you will lead will be perhaps a trifle less pleasant than the life of a parlor boarder in sheol.